Next Stop!

Next Stop!

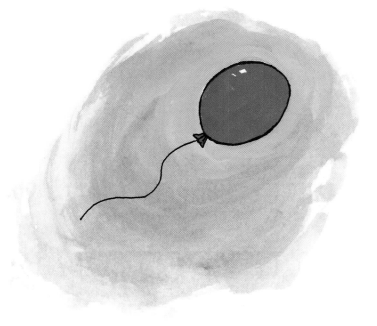

by Sarah Ellis

Illustrations by Ruth Ohi

Fitzhenry & Whiteside • Toronto

First published in the United States in 2000.

Fitzhenry & Whiteside acknowledges with thanks the Canada Council for the Arts,
the Government of Canada through the Book Publishing Industry Development Program (BPIDP),
and the Ontario Arts Council for their support of our publishing program.

Printed in Hong Kong.
Book Design by Wycliffe Smith.

10 9 8 7 6 5 4 3 2

Canadian Cataloguing in Publication Data

Ellis, Sarah
Next stop!

ISBN 1-55041-539-5

I. Ohi, Ruth. II. Title.

PS8559.57N49 2000   jC813'.54   C00-931782-1
PZ7.E4758Ne 2000

Dedication

For Nelson,
a reader in the making.

                                        —S.E.

───────────────────────────────────

Many thanks to the Toronto Transit Commission
and my models Quinlyn, John, Jeff and of course, Deb.

                                        —R.O.

On Saturday Claire rides the bus.
She sits right at the front. She helps the driver.
"Next stop, Moss Road," says the driver.

"Museum," says Claire.
"Ding," says the bell.

A bald man gets off.
A woman with many bags gets on.
"Next stop, James Street," says the driver.

"Ball park," says Claire.
"Ding," says the bell.

A girl with red hair gets off.
Three big kids get on.
"Next stop, Green Lane," says the driver.

"Shopping Mall," says Claire.
"Ding," says the bell.

A boy with rainbow shoes gets off.
A busy woman gets on. She is talking on a cell phone.
"Next stop, Eton Park Place," says the driver.

"Library," says Claire. "And?" says the driver.

"And Art gallery," says Claire.

"Ding, ding, ding," says the bell.

The three big kids get off. A baby gets on.
The baby is in a stroller. The stroller is pushed by a Dad.
"Next stop, McDonald Drive," says the driver.

"Hospital," says Claire.

"Ding," says the bell.

The woman with many bags gets off.
A dog with a man gets on.
"Next stop, Bank Avenue," says the driver.

"Stadium," says Claire.

"Ding," says the bell.

The dog and the man get off.
Five soccer players get on.
"Next stop, Long Court," says the driver.

"City Hall," says Claire.
"Ding," says the bell.
"Ring," says the cell phone.

The busy woman gets off.
A boy with a trombone gets on.
"Next stop, Robin Way," says the driver.

"College," says Claire. "And?" says the driver.
Claire just laughs.
The bell doesn't say anything.

Nobody gets off.

A smiling woman gets on.

The smiling woman kisses Claire.

The smiling woman is Claire's Mom.

The smiling woman kisses the bus driver.
The bus driver is Claire's Dad.

Everyone on the bus is smiling.

"Next stop, Peter Gardens,"
says the driver.

"Home!" says Claire.

"Home!" says Claire's Mom.

"Ding, ding," says the bell.